THE
STORY CLOUD

THE
STORY CLOUD

BY COOPER EDENS

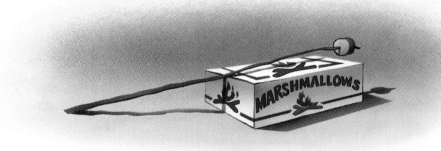

ILLUSTRATED BY
KENNETH LeROY GRANT

GREEN TIGER PRESS
Published by Simon & Schuster
New York London Toronto Sydney Tokyo Singapore

GREEN TIGER PRESS, Simon & Schuster Building, Rockefeller Center,
1230 Avenue of the Americas, New York, New York, 10020
Text copyright © 1991 by Cooper Edens
Illustrations copyright © 1991 by Kenneth Grant
All rights reserved including the right of reproduction
in whole or in part in any form.
GREEN TIGER PRESS is an imprint of Simon & Schuster.
Manufactured in the United States of America

10 9 8 7 6 5 4 3 2 1

Library of Congress Cataloging-in-Publication Data
Edens, Cooper.   The Story Cloud / by Cooper Edens :
illustrated by Kenneth LeRoy Grant. p.   cm.
Summary: Young Jimm travels to The Story Cloud,
where characters from fairy tales and other popular children's books reveal
to him the surprising truth about reality and the mystery of life.
[I. Characters and characteristics in literature—Fiction.]
I. Grant, Kenneth LeRoy, ill. II. Title. PZ7.S223Su 1991
[E]—dc20   91-13315

ISBN 0-671-74823-8

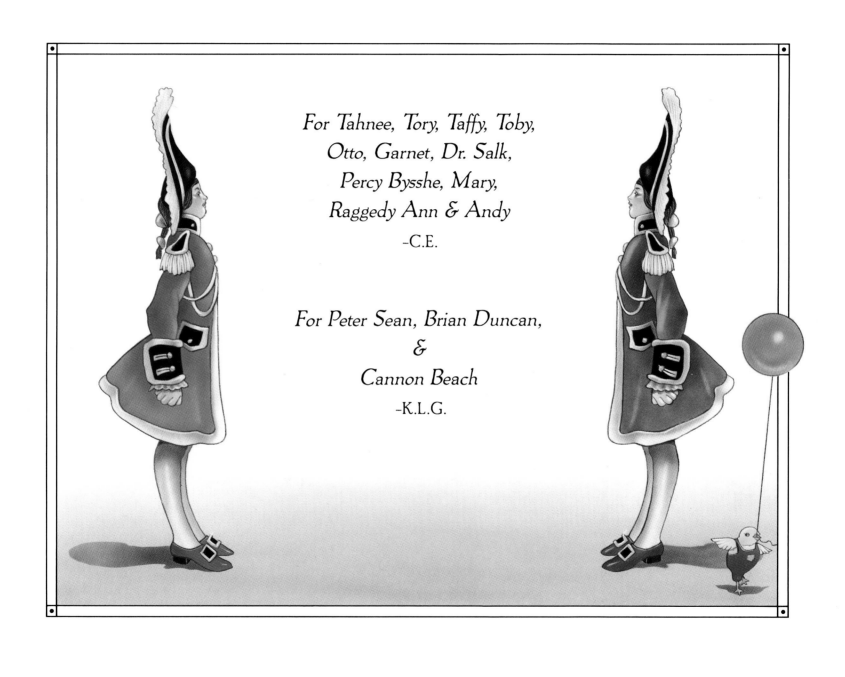

For Tahnee, Tory, Taffy, Toby,
Otto, Garnet, Dr. Salk,
Percy Bysshe, Mary,
Raggedy Ann & Andy
–C.E.

For Peter Sean, Brian Duncan,
&
Cannon Beach
–K.L.G.

THE
STORY CLOUD

It was the time of year I liked best, when winter turned to spring. I sang as I rode through the flower fields on my way to the beach. As I looked straight ahead a warm breeze blew across my face. Then it happened. There was something strange in the clouds.

When I came over the last hill, I saw the great
airship floating above the waves. It just hovered there,
silently... and though it looked transparent, what it
actually did was take on the appearance of whatever
its surroundings were at the time.

I put my bicycle on its kickstand and ran out onto the sand. In one of the airship's windows I was able to make out the friendly wave of a gloved hand. Then the door opened and I saw a boy clad in leaves, and a cat standing upright in a pair of boots with tassels and red scarlet heels.

"Young Jimm, come fly with us! We're bound for the top of the sky!" called out the boy, and the cat tossed down a rope ladder.

The cabin was filled with wondrous instruments—all embellished with gold, silver and jewels. At the controls were a man made of straw, a wooden puppet with a large twig nose, and a white rabbit with a waistcoat pocket and a large watch to put into it.

Outside the Earth was quickly flying back as the airship ascended.

"Amazing!" I suddenly shouted out, addressing nobody in particular.

"Why yes, Young Jimm," responded the white rabbit calmly. "And what you will find most admirable about 'the amazing' is that the amazing does not exist; all is true. All you are about to experience, Young Jimm . . . is wholeheartedly true."

Soon the Earth was a swirl of colors in the window beneath our feet. We had risen to the very edge of the sky. Then, just above us, I saw the perfect white cloud.

"There she is," the puppet said proudly of The Story Cloud, "she's the highest cloud in the sky!"

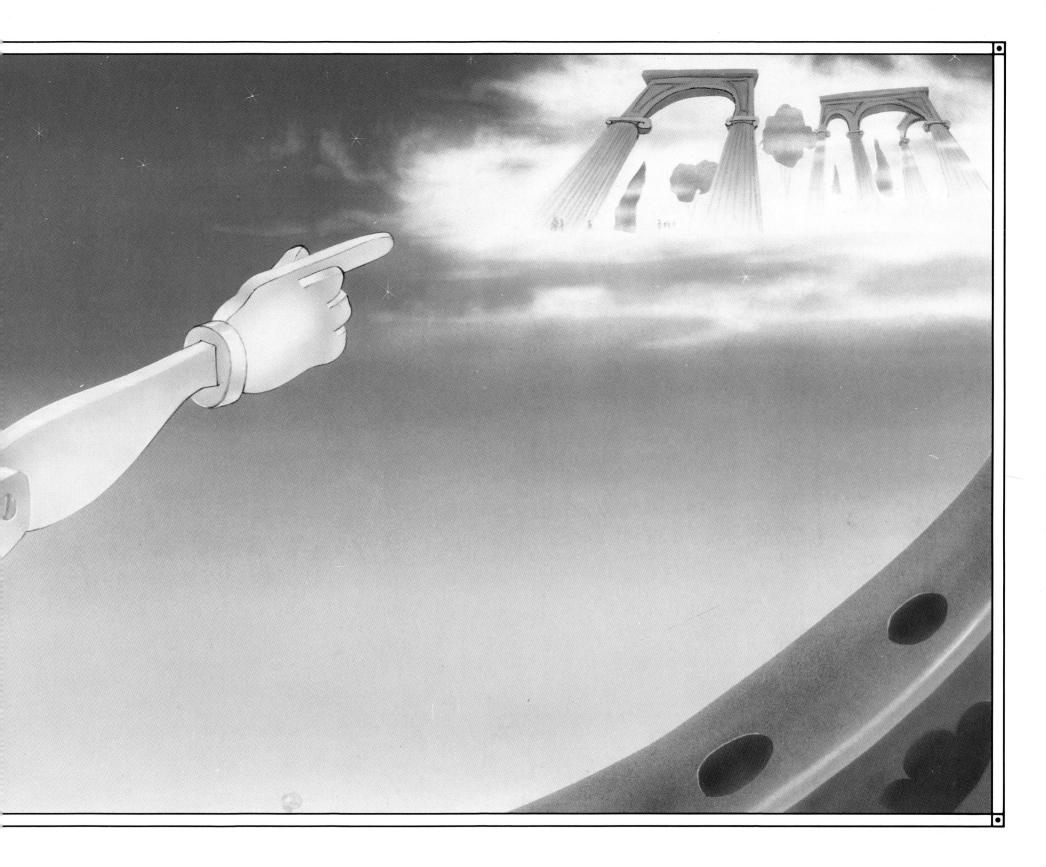

Then as we sailed into the cloud I saw that it had roads and villages, and that in one of the villages there was a square, and in that square a crowd was gathering.

"They're gathering to welcome you Young Jimm!" exclaimed the cat, waving his plumed hat with much excitement.

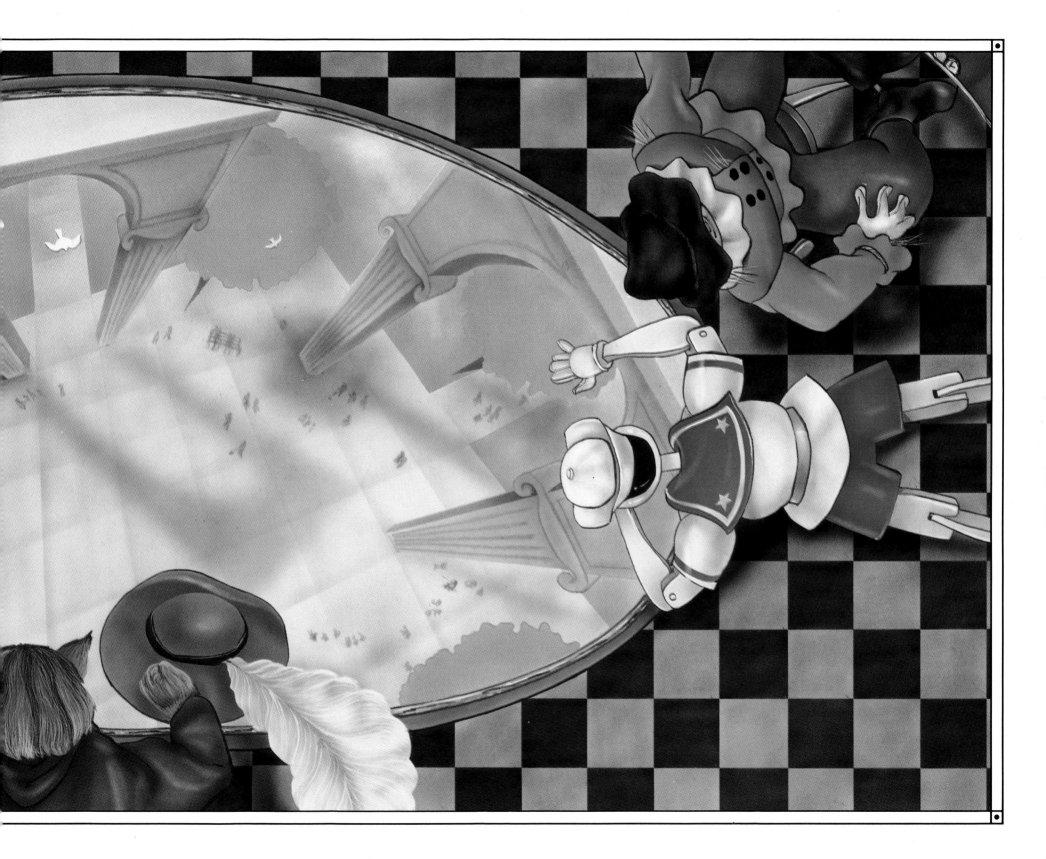

After we landed and the airship was secured, the puppet and the man made of straw ushered me to the door. What I saw was the most mysterious group of children, animals and creatures imaginable. Two young girls stepped forward to greet me with bouquets, while the others let balloons fly, threw confetti and waved enthusiastically in front of a beautifully hand-painted banner.

"I've fallen asleep and awakened in a dream," was all I could say.

"Dreams are real while they last, Young Jimm," replied the man made of straw in a strong passionate voice, "can you say any more of life?"

Almost immediately I found myself face to face with a gingerbread man, whose raisin eyes gleamed and whose little pink sugar mouth had been given the permanent shape of an "O".

"Oh my good fellow... the Princess is waiting, to escort you to the Ice," announced the cookie with an important air.

"The Ice?" I questioned politely, "What do you mean... to the Ice?"

"Oh dear and double dear... when you've survived as long as I have, you will learn that everything doesn't have to be explained!" the cookie replied rather loudly and he snapped his frosted fingers and instantly three little pigs appeared.

"The Princess is waiting!" the pigs sang out in unison.

"O.K., O.K., O.K.... then take Young Jimm away," chuckled the gingerbread man bouncing up into the air, "Oh gosh and double gosh, Oh golly and double golly, Oh gee and double gee!"

One of the three little pigs tucked his arm in mine and led me out through a short passage into a garden with bright flowerbeds and cool fountains.

Standing before us, in a long flowing gown, was the Princess.

"In this place Young Jimm," she began graciously, "reality is not always probable, or likely. So don't try looking for answers," she continued, as we followed her to the coach, "look instead, Young Jimm, for mysteries."

The coachman picked up his reins, the footmen blew their long horns and the coach began to move. The white wheels turned on the shiny cobblestones, where a light morning frost had just begun to melt. The coach rolled along on its reflection, the silent wheels spinning above and below, made no marks on the road. Slowly we wound up one terrace after another, and when the sun was shining directly overhead, we arrived at the Ice.

The Princess had the coachman pull right up in front of the Skate Rental Shop. The two young girls were already being fitted by a great, huge bear, a middle-sized bear and a little, small, wee bear.

When I approached the counter, a girl with golden locks was waiting with a pair of skates that were exactly my size.

"10¢ a day," is all she said, looking at me sweetly as she did so.

Unfortunately, I didn't have a cent and I was too shy to tell the girl. But to my good fortune... the seven tiny men, who were waiting in line behind me, sensed my predicament and were anxious to help.

"We'll be happy to give you this gold nugget in exchange for your high-top sneakers, Young Jimm," said the smallest of the small men.

Well, I loved my sneakers... but considering my circumstance, I gratefully accepted the little man's offer.

I was just beginning to lace up my skates when a little girl, peeping out from a red riding hood, tapped me on the shoulder.

"It's time for our picnic, Young Jimm," she said with a cheery tone, and she led me out onto the Ice. There she introduced me to her very unusual friend, who was standing at attention behind the most exquisite of sleighs.

"Hop right in, son," invited the wolf, so curiously clad in a grandmother's nightgown and cap, "It's my pleasure to chauffeur you around the Ice while you delight in a basketful of goodies."

While we picnicked, more and more Story Cloud Folk took to the Ice, and when we had finished our lunch, the little girl asked the wolf to position our sleigh where we were to witness, she proclaimed with great emphasis: "—quite an extraordinary ice show!"

When the music began, I was astounded by what I saw: a giant woodsman, while performing a death spiral, swung a great blue ox over his head... the seven tiny men formed a pyramid, where on top a lovely girl with skin as white as snow juggled apples... and above us, a cat with an eerie grin circled the Ice without skates, legs, or any evidence of a body at all!

After the peculiar follies ended, the little girl and the wolf took me to a marble courtyard at the center of the Ice. There they started a fire and unloaded boxes and boxes of marshmallows.

"It's time to tell stories!" the pair jubilantly announced, and they began the celebration by telling me their own odd tale. Then came, in turn, everyone I'd met or seen on The Story Cloud. The boy dressed in leaves told how he had never grown up, one of the young girls told of her adventures underground, and the other how there's no place like home. The stories were all incredible and I was entranced for hours and hours.

Finally, when there were only a few of us left around the fire, the dashing bowman, who had just told us about robbing from the rich to give to the poor, whispered to me as the man made of tin began the last story.

"Young Jimm, these stories belong to everyone. The fact that each and everyone's life is unique... means that each and everyone's life is identical. Listen to the man made of tin, for he is telling your story and mine."

The man made of tin finished his story by telling us how it felt when he first found his heart.

"I became transparent. As soon as I had a concern, I laughed at it . . . and all fear vanished from my joyful form," he said in a pleased tone, and we all clapped appreciatively.

Then a lion, who stood on his hind paws, stepped out from behind a column.

"Young Jimm, it is I the Princess has chosen to accompany you to the farthest reaches of The Story Cloud."

So I quickly laced up my skates, happy at last to have a chance to go *cloudskating*. As we started out, a tiny speck of brilliant light joined us and led us out into the great moonlit night.

"What is the meaning of all the stories?" I ventured to ask the lion, "and what was the purpose in telling them to me?"

"Well, Young Jimm, I'm glad you asked," replied the lion, in his humorous, yet sincere and rather drawn-out manner. "You see, once we believed what we were seeking was a meaning for life… but now we believe what we desire is the experience of being alive. We want to feel more fully the mystery of being alive, and by telling you our stories, Young Jimm, we are actually inviting you to return one day to tell us your story… which will, by being equally important and astonishing as our own, make our experience with life even more wonderfully mysterious."

And having said all that, he let out a mighty roar… and we skated on in a great hurry.

Soon we reached the most distant traces of The Story Cloud, where the Ice was at its thinnest. Waiting was the Princess, not in her beautiful gown, but dressed instead in a wretched threadbare jacket and a ragged frock, holding a broom. Her splendid coach, her white horses, her coachman and footmen had all disappeared. All that was beside her was a pumpkin, a number of mice, a rat, and a pair of lizards.

"As you can see, Young Jimm, it's quite late and time to get you home."

With that she took her broom and cleared frost from the Ice, so like a window we could look through. There below, to my surprise, was my house... but my parents' room was dark.

"Don't worry, Young Jimm," assured the Princess, "in our own way we have made sure your mother and father have not had a moment's concern about your whereabouts. They won't even have a question for you when you walk up the stairs to your room."

The lion then gave me a parachute and patting the top of my head with his paw, said:

"Remember, Young Jimm, as you grow older and the perils and promises of the years have all been attended to, and you turn to your heart—well, if you don't know where it is or what it is, believe me, you'll be sorry and, what's even worse, you'll be bored."

"That's true, Young Jimm," added the Princess, "if in your life you can put the news of the day and the problems of the hour into perspective, you will find your heart. And your heart will *be* your version of the whole story."

"But," I had to ask, "how will I put things into perspective?"

"When you desire *not* the meaning of life, but the mystery of life," she answered with pride and continued, "the mystery before you, the mystery to the left, the mystery above, the mystery to the right, and all around . . . you will be the beautiful story! You won't have to separate mystery from reality. Reality will be mystery. There will be no need of reality for you, Young Jimm."

And when she kissed me goodbye, I jumped and sailed through the morning light and thinking of her kiss . . . thought no more about The Story Cloud, or of anything else . . . that day, or the next.

Today at the age of 73, I am much too old to fool myself. So, I want the world to know... that I still believe there is a Story Cloud, and that as a small boy I was invited to spend a day there. Whether I was the only child ever to do so, or just one of a thousand, or a million... I have no way of knowing.

On the occasions when I have tried to ask others about their own such adventures, most just deny it... while others, who get a gleam in their eye, only quickly blink and change the subject.

As for the *things* I was told that day on The Story Cloud, well, the longer I live and the more I think about them... the more I believe them to be true.

You see, once we've found our heart and imagined ourselves... then the whole story plays like a big symphony, with everyone imagining everyone else... one great dream in which all the dream characters dream, too.

And what of my own dreaming? Well, my account of the story is beyond description—but I am compelled to tell it. And when the airship comes for me and I return to The Story Cloud, my wish is to sit around the campfire and share it.

❦ CAST of CHARACTERS ❦

The following is a list of characters,
in the order in which they appear in *The Story Cloud*,
attributing the character's earliest known mention in print.

The Scarecrow: *The Wonderful Wizard of Oz,* 1900, by L. Frank Baum

Peter Pan: *Peter Pan, or The Boy Who Wouldn't Grow Up,* 1902, by James M. Barrie

Puss in Boots: *Le piacevoli notti,* 1550, by Straparola

Pinocchio: *The Adventures of Pinocchio,* 1883, by Collodi

The White Rabbit: *Alice's Adventures in Wonderland,* 1865, by Lewis Carroll

Rapunzel: *German Popular Stories,* 1823, collected by The Brothers Grimm, from Oral Tradition

Rip Van Winkle: *Sketch Book of Geoffrey Crayon, Gent,* 1819, by Washington Irving

Little Boy Blue and Little Bo-peep: *Mother Goose Melodies,* 1833, anon.

Mr Toad: *The Wind in the Willows,* 1908, Kenneth Grahame

Jack and the Bean-Stalk: *Round About The Coal Fire,* 1734, anon.

Mr. Tiger: *The Story of Little Black Sambo,* 1899, Helen Bannerman

The Giant: *Round About The Coal Fire,* 1734, anon.

Alice: *Alice's Adventures in Wonderland,* 1865, by Lewis Carroll

Dorothy and Toto: *The Wonderful Wizard of Oz,* 1900, L. Frank Baum

Robin Hood: *A Lytell Geste of Robyn Hode,* 1510, anon.

Hansel and Gretel: *German Popular Stories,* 1823/26, collected by The Brothers Grimm, from Oral Tradition

Rumpelstiltskin: *Gargantua, Geschichtklitterung,* 1575, adapted by Johann Fischart, from Oral Tradition

Mother Goose: *Contes de ma mére l' Oye,* 1697, by Charles Perrault

The Tin Woodman: *The Wonderful Wizard of Oz,* 1900, L. Frank Baum

Sambo: *The Story of Little Black Sambo,* 1899, Helen Bannerman

The Catapillar: *Alice's Adventures in Wonderland,* 1865, by Lewis Carroll

The Little Red Hen: *Popular Rhymes and Nursery Tales,* 1849, collected by J. O. Halliwell

The Gingerbread Man: *English Fairy Stories,* 1890, anon.

The Three Little Pigs: *The Three Little Pigs,* 1853, collected by J. O. Halliwell

Cinderella, The Fairy Godmother, The Coachman, The Footmen, The Coach and The White Horses: *Histoires ou Contes du temps passè,* 1697, by Charles Perrault

The Three Bears: *The Doctor,* 1837, by Robert Southey

Goldilocks: *John Hassall's Nursery Stories and Rhymes,* 1904, adapted from R. Southey

The Seven Dwarfs: *Snowdrop, from German Popular Stories,* 1823, collected by The Brothers Grimm, from Oral Tradition

Little Red Riding Hood: *Histoires ou Contes du temps passè,* 1697, by Charles Perrault

The Hatter: *Alice's Adventures in Wonderland,* 1865, Lewis Carroll

Tom Thumb: *The History of Tom Thumb,* 1621, by Richard Johnson

Paul Bunyan and Babe the Blue Ox: *Paul Bunyan and His Big Blue Ox,* 1914, by W. B. Laughead, from Oral Tradition

Snow White: *Snowdrop, from German Popular Stories,* 1823, collected by The Brothers Grimm, from Oral Tradition

The Chesire Cat: *Alice's Adventures in Wonderland,* 1865, Lewis Carroll

Sleeping Beauty: *Histoires ou Contes du temps passè,* 1697, by Charles Perrault

Humpty Dumpty: *Mother Goose Melodies,* 1833, anon.

Tinkerbell: *Peter Pan, or The Boy Who Wouldn't Grow Up,* 1902, by James M. Barrie

The Cowardly Lion: *The Wonderful Wizard of Oz,* 1900, L. Frank Baum

The Pumpkin, The Rat, The Lizards and The Mice: *Histoires ou Contes du temps passè,* 1697, by Charles Perrault

The artist used airbrush and colored pencil
on Crescent illustration board.

The typeface is Packard and Packard Bold
set by SoCal Graphics of San Diego, California,

Designed by Judythe Sieck